Hello Kitty is...
Cinderella

First published in the UK by HarperCollins *Children's Books* in 2013

1 3 5 7 9 10 8 6 4 2

ISBN: 978-0-00-751997-2

Written by Neil Dunnicliffe

www.harpercollins.co.uk

Printed and bound in China

Hello Kitty is...
Cinderella

HarperCollins *Children's Books*

Hello Kitty is...

Cinderella

Dear Daniel is...

Prince Charming

Mimmy is...

the fairy godmother

Jody is...

Father

Cast

Tippy is...
Max

Fifi is...
Matilda

Tracy is...
the coachman

Thomas is...
the footman

Hello Kitty and her friends
are very excited. They are
acting in the school play.

The costumes are ready,
the cast have learned their
lines and the audience is
starting to arrive.

Ladies and gentlemen, girls
and boys, take your seats for...
Cinderella!

Once upon a time in the kingdom of Foreverland, there lived a beautiful young girl called Cinderella. She lived in a small cottage with her father, her step-brother, Max, and step-sister, Matilda.

Cinderella was very hard-working and did lots of the family's chores. She cooked and cleaned, tidied and washed – all without complaining.

Max and Matilda were kind-hearted and fun, but they could sometimes be a little naughty.

They loved to play tricks on Cinderella.

One day, there was a royal announcement.

Ta Da Da Daaaaa

The King was to hold a grand party at the royal palace for his son, Prince Charming.

Invitations arrived at the cottage for Max and Matilda, but it seemed there was nothing for Cinderella. She was very sad.

Every day Cinderella waited for the post, but a week passed and no invitation arrived. She wouldn't be going to the ball.

Cinderella didn't know that naughty Max and Matilda had hidden her invitation! They had meant to give it to her eventually, but had forgotten all about it.

The night of the ball arrived. Max and Matilda spent a long time getting ready.

Matilda chose a beautiful gown, a sparkling tiara and sequinned shoes.

Max put on his best suit and a bright red bow tie.

Max and Matilda went off to the ball. They wondered if they had forgotten something, but really couldn't remember what it was!

Cinderella was left at home, feeling sad. She decided to bake some chocolate cookies for everyone to eat when they returned.

Cinderella was just taking her chocolate cookies out of the oven when

Flash!

a fairy-like creature flew into the kitchen.

"Who are you?" asked Cinderella.

"I'm your fairy godmother. With my help, Cinders, you shall go to the ball!"

"But how? I have no time to get ready and no transport to take me there."

The fairy godmother asked Cinderella to fetch

a **pumpkin**
from the garden,

Max's four pet
white **mice**,

and Matilda's favourite
teddy bear.

How puzzling!

Maximus
Magicus

The fairy godmother waved her magic wand over the pumpkin, mice and teddy bear. Before Cinderella's eyes, they transformed into a glittering carriage with four white horses and a very dashing coachman.

"But I can't go the ball dressed like this," said Cinderella, looking at her flour-covered clothes.

Maximus Magicus

With a wave of her wand, the fairy godmother transformed Cinderella's outfit.

Suddenly she was wearing the most beautiful ballgown.
Cinderella looked down and saw delicate pink glass
slippers on her feet.

"Ensure you are home by midnight,"
said the fairy godmother.
"Any later and the spell will be broken."

When Cinderella arrived at the ball she was the most beautiful girl in the palace. She was dressed so finely that even Max and Matilda didn't recognise her.

When Prince Charming
saw Cinderella it was
love at first sight.

He asked her to dance and they waltzed
and quickstepped and jived all evening.

Suddenly the clock began to strike.

It was **midnight!**

"I must leave," Cinderella told the Prince. "Wait, please tell me your name," said Prince Charming, but it was too late.

Cinderella was gone. As she ran from the palace she lost one of her beautiful glass slippers.

The Prince picked up the slipper and carried it inside.

The next morning Prince Charming was feeling very sad. He had fallen in love with a beautiful girl, but had no clue who she was.

Then he looked at the dainty glass slipper and had an idea.

"I shall find the girl who owns this slipper."

He called his footman,

Footman!

and they rushed from the palace to begin the search.

After many hours, calling at every house in the land, the Prince had still not found the mystery girl. He was about to give up, when he saw one last cottage.

Bing Bong

went the doorbell.

Cinderella's father answered the door.

"Whosoever this shoe fits, I shall marry," said the Prince.

Matilda rushed forward and tried on the slipper, but it was much too small for her.

Even Max tried on the shoe, but his foot was much too big!

The Prince then noticed Cinderella, busy doing chores. She stepped forward and tried on the slipper.

It was a perfect fit!

Cinderella would marry the Prince!

Ding Dong Ding Dong went the church bells.

Cinderella looked wonderful dressed in her wedding gown.
Standing by her side was Prince Charming,
her new husband.

"We're so sorry we hid your invitation to
the ball," said Matilda and Max.
"Please don't worry," said Cinderella,
as she smiled for the photographer.

Flash!

Princess Cinderella enjoyed life at the palace. From time to time she still baked her favourite cookies. They became Prince Charming's favourites too!

The Prince and Princess lived happily ever after.

The End

Hooray! Hooray!

Cheers are ringing around the hall,
as the audience claps and shouts for more.

The play is a great success. The friends take a bow and
Hello Kitty receives a beautiful bouquet of flowers.

Hello Kitty looks at Dear Daniel across
the stage. "Maybe one day," she thinks,
"I will marry *my* prince."